A Tale of Two Slugs

by Sydnie Meltzer Kleinhenz
illustrated by Eldon Doty

Scott Foresman

Editorial Offices: Glenview, Illinois • New York, New York
Sales Offices: Reading, Massachusetts • Duluth, Georgia
Glenview, Illinois • Carrollton, Texas • Menlo Park, California

A big slug slid out from under a pile of wet leaves and onto the porch step. A little slug followed close behind.

"Caution! Danger zone!" yelled the little slug, but the big one kept going. "Stop, Squig! You know what the wise old slugs say."

"Learn the slime tales, Buddy," said Squig. He continued to push forward.

"It's true about humans," Buddy said.
"They can make us as flat as a mat with
one step. How can little one-footed slugs
get away from their two big feet?"

Squig slowed down. "I'm hunting for a
little adventure, and this looks like a good
place to find it. I promise I'll keep my eyes
open for humans."

He started up the shoe.

Buddy felt the ground shake. He swung his eyes and saw the thing that he feared most.

"Squig, don't! Stop!" Buddy yelled as he scooted to catch Squig. At that moment, a human's fingers lifted the shoe, leaving Buddy dangling from Squig's foot.

"Buddy! I'm glad you stuck around,"
Squig said as he was enjoying the ride.

Buddy squirmed closer. "I'm trying to
save you, Squig."

Squig shrugged his feelers. "I thought
you were telling me, 'Don't stop!'"

The slugs rode into the house on the
side of a soccer shoe.

The shoe landed on the floor and the woman left.

"I'm hungry. Let's see if this place has leaves," Squig said. He and Buddy made sparkling slime trails as they slid.

"We have to go home," Buddy said. "You know what the wise old slugs say. 'Don't go sticking your feelers into other folks' business.'"

"You're still little. Children have much to learn," said Squig. "I've been around two summers, so you can trust me. I know we'll be fine."

"Feet! Feet!" Buddy yelled as the floor
shook. The slugs scrunched up their bodies
to look as small as possible.

A boy ran in and grabbed a dog bone
on the floor. The dog barked and danced
around, knocking the shoes over.

The boy tossed the bone out the
doorway and raced with his dog to get it.

Squig poked one eye out from under a
shoe and looked around. He tapped Buddy
with a feeler. "We're fine," he said.

"We have to go home," Buddy said.

"Which way is home?" Squig said
looking and feeling. "We might be close.
I see some twigs."

Squig slid onto the pretzel sticks.
"What's this stuff on the twigs?" he asked.
Buddy saw some loose crystals and
yelled, "Salt! You know what the wise
old slugs say."

"I know, I know," said Squig, who had
fallen on his side and begun to shake.
"Salt will dry up your slime. It will dry
you up too!"

"Squig, I'll help you," said Buddy.
"You're too little," Squig whispered.

"You need water, quick," Buddy said as he looked high and low. "I see some water. Come on Squig."

"I can't move, Buddy. It burns," cried Squig.

Squig was big, but he didn't have much sticky slime left. Buddy rolled him over and over to the water on the floor near the dog's bowl.

Squig stopped talking. His body was curled up and still. Buddy dipped his feelers in the water and patted them on Squig. Slowly Squig stretched.

Buddy sighed and blinked his blurry eyes. "Get back up on your foot," he begged Squig. "We have to go home."

"How?" Squig asked weakly.

Buddy had to think for a moment. Then he softly spoke the answer to Squig's question. "The wise old slugs say, 'Go back the way you came.'"

Suddenly, the floor shook.

Buddy and Squig froze. They watched
the human bend down to the floor and
blink its eyes near their eyes.

Buddy sighed. Squig wailed, "Now
what do we do?"

The woman squealed. "Slugs! Gross! I
have to get rid of them. I need something
to pick them up." Her big feet shook the
floor as she left the room.

"Crank up the slime," Buddy ordered.
"Move quickly!"

Buddy and Squig slid to the shoes as
fast as they could.

"How can this work?" asked Squig.

"Do as the wise old slugs say," panted
Buddy. Suddenly he saw the shoes in a
new way. "Follow me," he told Squig.

Buddy scooted between the bumps on
the bottom of the shoe. "The human is on
our trail so we have to hide," said Buddy.

A boy walked into the room.

"Hurry!" Buddy said. "Squeeze in!"
Squig didn't have the breath to answer.

They had just slipped out of sight
when the boy sat on their slime trails.
He quickly put on his soccer shoes, and
jumped up.

"See you later, Mom. I'm going to the
field to play soccer," he said.

"Bye," said the mom. Then she bent
down to the floor. "Now where did those
slugs go? Their trails just stop!"

The boy's feet pounded the ground as
he ran on out the door onto the porch.
There, he stopped to zip his jacket.

"Let's get out of here!" Buddy said.

The slugs got their feet on the ground
only moments before the boy ran down
the steps.

Buddy and Squig slid off the porch. They hurried under the leaves in the garden.

"Whew!" Squig said. "We're safe!"

"You know what the wise old slugs say," Buddy said. " 'Better safe than squashed!' "

"That was too much of an adventure for me," Squig said.

Buddy took a bite of a green leaf. "Let's just hunt leaves," he said between chews.

Squig laughed. "Okay, Boss. I'll take mine unsalted!"